Sharing is Fun

for Everyone!

Shirley Ann Bivens

D1275460

Dedication

This is my first children's book, and I'd like to dedicate this book
to my beautiful, wonderful, Italian Mother, Frances—
who always modeled generosity for me, and graciously showed
me with love how to share, and what "fun it is for everyone!"

But do not forget to do good and to share, for with such sacrifices God is well pleased.

Hebrews 13:16

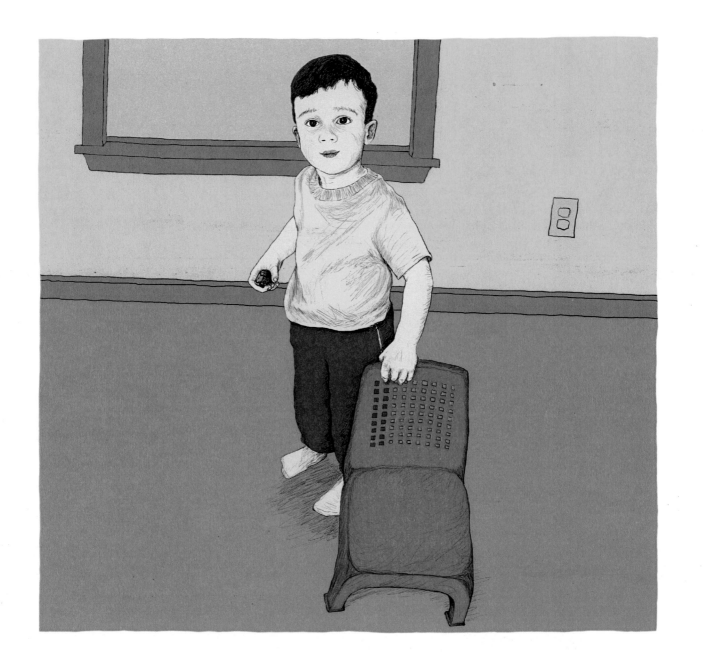

I like to share my little red chair.

I like to share my fuzzy bear.

I like to share it shows I care.

Coco the clown likes to share...

animal balloons filled with air.

I like to share the brush for my hair...

with my little brown bear.

I like to share with my cats
when they sleep in the chair.

When they wake up to play
they are quite a pair.

I like to share my favorite ball
with my sister Claire.

I like to share it shows I care.

I like to share the clothes I wear.

I like to share but not my underwear!

I like to share apples with the mare.

It's fun to share, it shows I care.

I like to share our times of prayer.

Mommy and daddy like to share
when they swing me in the air.

Jesus smiles when he sees me care.
He loves it when His ways I share.
God shared His son
when He had only one.
He shared His best for everyone.

We can give Him our best too.
It's fun, it's fun and easy too.

The Colors Used in this Book

	White / Black	
	Green / Yellow	
	Orange / Blue	
	Light Blue / Purple	
	Tan / Brown	
	Gray / Beige	
	Pink / Red	

Everything colored RED is what's shared.

The words that rhyme with "Share"

Chair

Bear

Care

Air

Hair

Pair

Claire

Wear

Underwear

Mare

Prayer

SHIRLEY ANN BIVENS resides in a small town in Southern Pennsylvania. She lives with her husband of over 40 years in an old house nestled within the Blue Mountain range. The Mother of two awesome "grown children," she is also a joyful "Grammy" to five amazing smaller ones. She has taught Christian pre-school for over 13 years, and has always had a deep love and tender heart for children.

Although children have taken up a large part of her life and her heart, Jesus is her first love and she has a passion for telling others about Him. Her platform for doing this is in clown ministry. For over 30 years she has had the pleasure of spreading the gospel message to children and adults as CoCo the clown.

Sharing is Fun for Everyone! is her first children's book and her hope is that it inspires and teaches "everyone" the good and Godly joy of giving.

Contact Information

If you would like to contact Shirley to speak on "sharing"
and read her book to your preschool, sunday school, or Kindergarten class;
or if you need to contact her for the copying of the images in this book;
you can email her at: shirleybivens@gmail.com.

Donations from this book will go to support
ministries that fight child sex-trafficking.

To order more copies of this
book please go to:

www.createspace.com/4724529

Made in the USA
Middletown, DE
12 January 2015